Dònal Òg and the Shaking Bog

BOOK FOUR OF THE DÒNAL ÒG SERIES

by

Donal McCarthy

Illustrations by Emily Fuhrer

Website: **DonalOgSeries.com**

Joshua Tree Publishing

• Chicago •

Dònal Òg and the Shaking Bog
BOOK FOUR OF THE DÒNAL ÒG SERIES

by Donal McCarthy

Published by
Joshua Tree Publishing
• Chicago •
JoshuaTreePublishing.com

13-Digit ISBN: 978-1-956823-06-6

Credits: All Illustrations by Emily Fuhrer
Website: **DonalOgSeries.com**

Disclaimer:

Printed in the United States of America

Dedication

*To my daughters
Cara, Ashling, and Níamh
and my grandaughters
Eden and Aria*

Thank You
Emily Fuhrer
Ami on Vancouver Island
John Paul Owles

Dònal Òg and the Shaking Bog

Dònal Òg loved the summer holidays, nine long weeks with no grouchy teachers or hours of homework in the evenings. He could lie in bed in the morning without worrying about being late for school. He would hear pots rattling downstairs as Ma made breakfast, as well as the sound of the kettle boiling on the hearth, sending the message that tea would soon be ready. It was time to climb out of bed and get ready to face the day and whatever adventures it brought.

On winter nights, as he lay in bed, listening to the river roaring past on its way to join the far-off sea, he imagined longboats full of marauding Vikings as they sped along looking for the next settlement to rob and plunder.

He was glad that they had a treaty with the fairy king to protect them from the Vikings. At least, that's what Da told him when he cried out in fear in the darkness. When he looked the next morning to see if they had left anything behind while they were passing, he was amazed to see it wasn't a big river at all, just a small stream that ran softly between its banks. Then he understood how the fairies protected them. They put a spell on the river and made it so small that the Vikings' longboats couldn't fit on it.

From the front garden, Dònal Òg looked straight out over the bog onto the green fields in the distance. On a hilltop stood the fairy fort. Not far from it was the enchanted woods, the home of a family of walking, talking trees. These were cousins to Dharaig, the king of all the walking trees, whom Dònal Òg had met on his last adventure with Eden and Aria.

Far away on the horizon stood the highest mountains in Ireland. It was often snow-capped in winter, but now in summer, they glowed purple in the early morning light. As the sun rose over the hills behind him, the light touched the tops of the mountain peaks. It flowed down all the way until it reached the valley below and then raced back to him across the fields. In front of the house between the road and the bog was a small, fast-flowing stream. It was a perfect place for leaf or twig races or for catching small fish with hands cupped. So amidst all this beauty and perfection, why was there a frown on Dònal Òg's face?

The answer to that question is staring him right in the face. It was THE BOG! Or, to be more specific, THE SHAKING BOG. It had such a fearsome reputation that everybody avoided it. Animals were fenced off from entering it. Children were totally forbidden to even look over the ditch at it or even THINK of going anywhere near it. It was so unstable that even the fairies couldn't walk on it (and we all know that fairies weigh less than butterflies). It was a lonely area left to the wild birds, curlews, snipes, corncrakes, and the occasional herons. They were light enough and fast enough to explode into flight the moment they got that sinking feeling.

So the bog lay there, feeling lonely, cut off from contact with all other creatures. It would tremble when it heard footsteps on the road or felt the vibrations of the pounding of the horses' hooves as they raced along over the fields. The bog understood why everyone was so afraid of him, and he couldn't blame them—not everyone was as touchy-feely as he was. He was so overcome with love and emotion when anything touched him that he just wrapped his arms around them in a big hug with disastrous results. He thought perhaps he should never hug a big bull again, no matter how lonely he felt. That last one left him feeling bloated and very gassy.

What do these creatures eat? he thought. It was dreadful, especially as he couldn't hold his nose.

Unaware of the turmoil going on in the mind of the shaking mass on the other side of the hedge, Dònal Òg set about working out how he and his cousins Eden and Aria could get to the enchanted forest with the least amount of effort. They could walk down the dusty road to the bridge, then walk along the banks of the Doughlasha until they came to the meadow that was right alongside the bog and walk up the hill until they reached the entrance to the enchanted woods. Maybe they could catch a fish that would make them more clever when they ate it.

He didn't believe Eden and Aria when they said their mom had given them a lot of it to eat already. He was cleverer than they were, and he hadn't even seen one.

They might be able to find a snipe's nest and see the eggs. He wanted to show his cousins what color they had. When he told them that they were olive-colored with brown markings and that the mallard's eggs were greenish-blue, they didn't believe him.

"Eggs are either white or brown," said bossy Miss Eden.

"Everyone knows that," said her shadow, Aria.

Dònal Òg believed that his Da was the most clever man in the whole world. Da always said that an empty bucket made the most noise. Dònal Òg had never understood what Da meant until he met his two cousins. Everything Dònal Òg told his cousins was treated with disbelief. They questioned it until they were satisfied, and they never apologized when he turned out to be correct. He was seven years old and knew so many things. His cousins came from a place far, far away that didn't have any of the things he had. No fairies, no forts, no magic forests, no enchanted woods, no trolls.

He even had to show them that the milk they drank in their tea came from a cow.

"Ewww," said Eden.

"Gross!" Aria said. "You are wrong. It came from a tall metal container." She had seen it with her very own eyes where they bought it back home. Thank you very much!

Then Dònal Òg had an idea on how to get his cousins to the other side of the bog. He would climb up one of the small trees, tie a rope to the very top, and pull the tip right down to the ground. Then he would tie the girls (one at a time) to the top of the tree, cut the rope, and fire them right over the bog where they would land in the green field on the other side.

Overcome with his own brilliance, he set about putting his plan into action. He found a long rope. Unfortunately, it was around the neck of the nanny goat and tied to a tree to stop it from chasing everyone. This was a setback, no doubt about that. But he was a clever, brave fellow. He thought he just had to find a solution. And find one he did!

From the shed, he took a few carrots. Then he stood behind the gate and waved them at the nanny goat. It spied them and charged straight at Dònal Òg. Its head flew straight through the bars, barely missing him as he jumped back.

With its head firmly trapped, he removed the rope and ran as fast as he could before it got its head free and charged him again. Escaping over the wall with a second to spare, he stopped and threw a rock at the nanny goat. He didn't even leave it a carrot. It glared after him, promising to get revenge.

Finding the right tree was a bigger problem. It had to be near the bog but out of sight of the cottage. If Ma saw what he was doing, she would put a stop to it. She was always spoiling his brightest ideas.

After searching for a little while, he found the perfect tree, just the right height and thickness for his plan. He climbed right to the top (almost) and threw the rope down. Then realizing that he hadn't tied it to the tree, he had to scramble back down again to fetch it. Climbing back up was not as easy the second time. *This is hard work*, he thought.

Finally, there he was, nearly at the top of the tree. Looking around, he thought that it was a long way up from the ground. He could see the enchanted forest and the fairy fort in the distance. The bog looked a lot smaller than from the ground. The river seemed to have shrunk as well. He wondered if perhaps the fairies were putting a spell on him, so he clambered back down quickly.

Yes, he thought, everything is back to normal. I got out of there just in time.

Safely back on the ground, he put his plan in motion. Finding the rope, he began pulling the tip downward. After a lot of huffing and puffing, he had it just in the right position to tie it down. Looking around for something to tie it to, he thought that perhaps he should have done that before all the hard work of pulling it down. Spying a perfect tree to tie it to, he pulled the rope in that direction. No use. He tried as hard as he might, but it was just a tiny bit too short. *Very frustrating*, he thought.

Just then, out of the corner of his eye, he saw a white shape hurtling toward him, head-down. It was the nanny goat full of evil intent! No longer tied down, it was free to roam wherever it wished. The nanny goat wished to be right where it was right now, on its way to punish Dònal Òg for his transgressions.

Letting go of the rope just in time, Dònal Òg scrambled up the nearest tree out of reach of the vengeance, thundering past not three feet away from his feet. The nanny goat stopped in confusion. *How do humans disappear just like that?* the nanny goat wondered and left.

Holding on to the tree for all he was worth, Dònal Òg looked at the rope now hanging straight down from the once-more-upright tree. He thought of all the hard work gone to waste. He said all the rude words he knew and then looked around in case Ma might have heard him. He was forbidden to use any of those words and would be punished if she heard him. Luckily for him, she was nowhere nearby, so he was saved.

This time, he searched for somewhere to tie the rope to first. Finding the right spot, he started all over again, keeping one eye out for the goat. He pulled with all his might, and finally, it was done. He looked at his masterpiece with great pride. He visualized tying the turkey to the tip of the tree to make sure it would work as he imagined it would.

"Only a clever man can think of this," he said. "Maybe in the future, this will be how people travel over long distances. No more having to walk or travel over bumpy roads—just fly through the air, and in no time, you are at your destination. I will keep this a secret until I find a plan on how to do it for everyone. I can make a lot of money. Da won't have to work anymore."

His tummy was now grumbling, so he ran home for something to eat. Entering the kitchen, he found Aria and Eden sitting at the table. Ma had made a big pot of soup. A plate of thick-cut crusty bread slathered with butter sat on the table. Soon they were all munching away happily.

"What shall we do this afternoon?" asked Eden. "I feel like doing another adventure."

Aria looked at Dònal Òg and said, "I am sure you have planned a big surprise for us."

"Yes, I have," he said. "Follow me." He led them to where he had prepared his tree catapult, explaining to them what he had in mind. He invited them to lie on the tree where he could tie them down. They looked at him as if he was crazy.

"No way!" they said. "Why don't we tie you to the tree, and we will catapult you over the swamp?"

It was now his turn to disagree. "Not possible!" he said. "Only a boy is strong enough to loosen the rope. It's tied too tight."

They argued back and forth for the longest time, but neither would give in. In the end, Aria said, "I know. Let's catch a turkey and see if it works on that. If it does, we can always pull straws to see who goes first."

They caught a turkey but then found that they didn't have anything to tie it down with.

"Let's use my belt," said Eden, so they did. The complaining turkey was tied to the tip of the tree. Then the rope was untied, and the tree flew upright with a loud whoosh. It continued to whip back and forth for quite some time. A few feathers floated down and then quite a few more.

Trying as hard as they could, they couldn't see where the turkey had landed. Dònal Òg scrambled up the tree to see if he could see from there.

"It must have flown right into the fairy fort!" he said. "We will never see it again."

As he got close to the top, he became aware of a loud complaining coming from above his head. There sat a very enraged turkey, completely shaken up and ready to show its displeasure with pecking beak and flying spurred feet. Being tied down meant, of course, that it couldn't become a flying projectile. It just whipped back and forth, half-naked, until the tree quietened down again.

"This is a fine pickle," thought Dònal Òg as he tried to untie the angry turkey. It pecked him many times before he was able to free it. Then it disappeared down the tree and staggered back to the cottage, weaving its way all around the garden.

By now, it was getting late, and Da would be home soon. Dònal Òg had to get the rope back on the nanny goat before Da discovered it wandering around or, even worse, being attacked by the crazy creature. Not being the cleverest creature in creation, the nanny goat once again fell for the carrot-and-gate trick. Soon it had the rope back around its neck, much to its disgruntlement.

Ma was standing in the backyard, scratching her head, and saying to no one in particular, "I think that turkey is ready for the oven. It's waltzing around the yard as if it's drunk."

As if to agree with her, the turkey stumbled past her, looking for all the world like the postman on Christmas Eve. The three children pretended not to see anything as they sped off down the field to play in the river.

Not long after, Ma was calling everyone home for supper. As they sat around the table, Da asked what they had been doing all day.

"Not much," they said, "just playing."

Ma mentioned that the nanny goat and one of the turkeys both seemed out of sort.

"Must be the weather," said Da. "The heat does that to them."

They all agreed. Soon it was time for bed. Tomorrow was another day.

Sleep didn't come quickly to Dònal Òg, and when it did, it was a very restless one.

Ma came into his room, telling him, "Your head is getting too big. Don't be such a big shot all the time. You are fighting with your lovely cousins Eden and Aria and upsetting them."

Then both of his cousins were standing next to his bed, saying, "Yes, smarty-pants, you think you know everything better than us. If we had listened to your stupid idea about the tree, we would have been hurt badly."

To make matters even worse, he found himself in the yard. The nanny goat and the half-naked turkey began to chase him all around. He ran as fast as his legs could carry him, shouting for Ma to save him.

He woke up with Da shaking him, saying, "It's just a bad dream. Everything is okay."

His heart was pounding like the hooves of a running horse. His mouth was as dry as when he ate some of Godmother Gracie's ginger cake. Da brought him a glass of water and told him to go back to sleep. He told him the fairies would watch over him. When Da was gone, he jumped out of bed and checked the size of his head in the mirror. He thought it might be looking a bit bigger and decided there and then not to be cocky anymore and to be nice to Eden and Aria. Feeling much better having made the decision, he went back to bed and was soon sleeping soundly.

The next morning, he bounded out of bed as soon as he heard Ma working in the kitchen. Running to the bathroom, he checked his head in the mirror again. He still thought it looked a bit swollen and promised himself again that he would work on quickly getting it back to its normal size. As they all sat around the breakfast table, he kept expecting Ma or Aria and Eden to say something about it but was happy when they didn't seem to notice. With breakfast sitting happily in their tummies, they all ran out of the house to play.

"What adventure should we have today?" Dònal Òg asked the girls. He thought he felt his head getting a tiny bit smaller. *Being nice isn't all that hard*, he thought. *I will make sure to be like this all the time.*

The girls were happy to be asked. They were a bit fed up with being told what to do all the time. "Let's go to the enchanted woods," they both said in unison, "but let's take the route along the riverbank and through the meadow." They didn't want a repeat of yesterday's exercise.

Dònal Òg quickly agreed. He admitted to himself that it wasn't one of his best ideas but still felt it had potential as soon as he had worked out the few small kinks in the plan. He thought that the next time he would tie the goat to the tree with a light rope, not a belt. Combining the weight of the goat and the weakness of the rope, he was sure the rope would snap once it reached the apex. Then the goat would definitely sail over the bog.

Walking to the bridge, they climbed down to the riverbank and followed it along until they reached the green field.

A cock pheasant exploded out from under their feet, scaring them half to death. Ducks quacked their way along the stream as they floated past. Every now and again, they stuck their heads underwater and their bottoms in the air. They were eating underwater. A large brown trout watched them from under a bush that hung out over the water. It swished its tail and fins, but they never saw it.

Further along stood a large gray heron staring fixedly at the exact spot where the trout lay. It had seen a ripple in the water but wasn't sure. It could afford to stay motionless for as long as it took. It had just devoured a large fat frog and was feeling quite pleased with life.

They watched as a damselfly, checking on where it had deposited its eggs, flew too close to the water. The trout burst through the surface and devoured it before it had a chance to blink an eye, just four gossamer wings floating along to show that it had ever existed.

"Naughty fish!" shouted Aria.

"I hope that the big gray bird eats you," said Eden.

And then that's exactly what happened: the heron covered the ground even before the trout had landed back in the water. Before it knew what was happening, it had been impaled on the long sharp bill and flung in the air and had disappeared down the throat of the happy bird. Dònal Òg thought he was glad that he wasn't a fish or an insect. The heron burped and flew away with a heavy wingbeat. *I have to come here again*, it thought. *I like the menu.*

As they skirted the bog by walking through the green field, they chatted happily about all their adventures. They were excited about visiting the enchanted woods and hoped that the walking, talking trees would reveal themselves to them. Not all trees were enchanted, only a few. Most of the trees were normal trees—ash, beech, and sycamore. Enchanted trees were usually oaks, hawthorn, or rowan trees.

Soon they stood at the entrance and peered in. Remembering their manners, they called out loudly, "Please may we enter your home? We are from the cottage across the fields and would like to come and play."

There was no answer, but they imagined that they could see eyes watching them. They quietly entered and walked around. Over there in the corner stood a crab apple tree laden with the reddest, smallest perfect apples that they had ever seen.

"Yummy!" shouted Aria. "Let's try one. They look delicious."

"No," said Dònal Òg. "They are for the fairies only. If we eat them, we become enchanted and might never be able to find our way out of these woods again."

What a bummer, Eden thought but didn't say anything in case the fairies heard.

They looked around all over the woods. They saw rabbits, foxes, a lot of different birds, some squirrels, and a family of red deer. Soon they felt tired from all the walking and running and sat down under a huge chestnut tree. They felt safe and happy there. It was so quiet that they could hear the sound of the birds' wings as they flew from tree to tree. They could hear all the way across the field and bog to the cottage, hearing Ma singing as she fed the chickens. They smiled and fell asleep.

Eden woke first to the sound of giggling. When she opened her eyes just the tiniest bit, she saw three baby trees slowly moving toward them. They were lifting their small roots very gently out of the earth and gliding closer. Eden touched both Aria and Dònal Òg and softly said, "Don't move or call out. We are being approached by three moving baby trees."

They watched from under hooded lids as the trees looked closely at them, all the time chattering away among themselves. "What strange creatures," they were saying. "What are they doing here in our woods?"

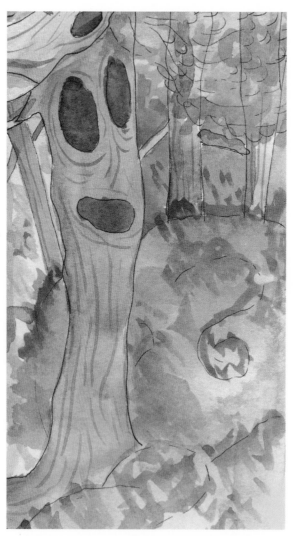

Aria started to softly sing a sweet song about how beautiful the woods were and how pretty the trees were. She had a lovely voice. The little trees were enchanted by her lovely voice. Then Eden stood up and performed a dance. Not knowing what to do, Dònal Òg broke wind, much to the disgust of Eden and Aria.

The little trees gathered around them as Eden and Aria told them stories of their lives outside the enchanted woods. The little trees were delighted. They found their lives in the woods very boring, nothing to do for years at a time but stand around. A loud gasp startled them all. There stood a magnificent rowan tree dressed up with its beautiful mantle of elongated green leaves and clusters of red berries.

"What a beautiful tree!" said both girls at the same time. "It's the prettiest tree we have ever seen."

Of course, the rowan tree was flattered—who wouldn't be? And before realizing it, the tree had said, "Thank you very much!"

It hadn't meant to reveal itself to the children, but it was too late to retreat now. So she welcomed the children to her woods. She explained that she was the ruler of the enchanted woods and that Dharaig was a relative from many long years ago. Her kind had lived in these lands long before the fairies or humans. She explained that the woods had covered the entire island of Ireland in olden times. Wild red deer and wolf had run free, and the fox and badger had roamed in their thousands. Then humans arrived, and it was all downhill from there. It was the same story that Dharaig had told the children.

The rowan continued, "Look down there." She pointed with her branch to the shaking bog. "Many years ago, that was beautiful woodland just like here. Then the humans cut down all the trees and blocked the streams. With no trees to drink the water and nowhere for the water to run to, it just sank into the ground until it became saturated and drowned. Now nothing can grow there or walk on it without dying."

Dònal Òg was listening very carefully. "Do you mean that if the streams were opened again, the water would flow away, and the bog could stop shaking and become safe?"

"Yes," said the rowan. "It would have to be done very carefully. You can't let all the muddy water run into the river at once. The mud will fill the river and kill every breathing thing in it. Then it will become another shaking bog! But it can be done if it's done slowly. Divert the water into the drainage ditches that run between the bog and the fields. The mud will stay in the ditch, and the water will enter the river eventually, still a little brown but full of nutrients that are good for all the living creatures in it and along its banks."

The children could hear Ma calling them from the front of the cottage. Saying their goodbyes, they thanked the rowan and her children for a lovely visit. Promising to come again, they sped down the hill to home.

Dònal Òg couldn't wait to tell Da what the tree had told him. Da often suspected that he suffered from an overactive imagination but listened anyway. *Better let the lad let off steam*, he thought, *than keep these things in his head.*

Later that week, Da talked to the farmer that owned the field. "Have you ever thought of draining the bog?" he asked him.

The farmer was noncommittal until Da said, "Can you imagine being able to cut hay in a big field here instead of losing cows, sheep, and horses in it? If you drain the bog into the ditches before it gets to the river, you can shovel the mud back out and use it as fertilizer instead of having to pay for it in town!"

That sounded much better to the farmer. "You are full of brilliant ideas," he said to Da. "I should pay you to dig the drainage ditches for me." And that's what he did!

Over the next few months, Da labored mightily. He dug several trenches from the bog into drainage ditches. The water slowly seeped out from under the bog until it was soon safe to walk on it. Not long after, it was as dry as any field in the parish.

The bog got a whole new lease on life. It was now a happy and smiling field. Children came to play on it.

Birds, damsel flies, bees, and other animals visited all the time. With so much nutrient-rich water flowing in the river, the fish got bigger and bigger, and the frogs became as big as dinner plates.

The herons grew so large that they could no longer fly, so they walked everywhere. Dònal Òg decided to capture a few and use them to pull the cart as they couldn't afford a pony like his cousins.

And that's what he set out to do.

But that's a story for another day.

The End

READ THE DÒNAL ÒG SERIES

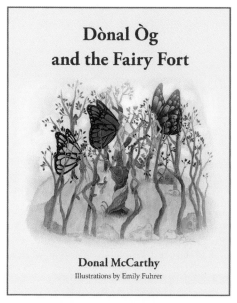

BOOK ONE

BOOK TWO

Dònal Òg is a young boy growing up in the rural Irish countryside in the 1950s. These are the tales that were told in front of a glowing peat fire that the family would gather around on the dark winter nights. It was before the invention of television, so people made their own entertainment. Belief in the fairy folk was strong amongst the people, especially the children. The tales carried many suggestions on how to behave and included many warnings on the consequences of breaking those rules. As a boy with a very active imagination, **Dònal Òg** took it all to heart.

These are his stories.

Website: DonalOgSeries.com

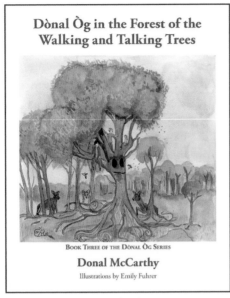

Dònal Òg in the Forest of the
Walking and Talking Trees

BOOK THREE OF THE DÒNAL ÒG SERIES

Donal McCarthy

Illustrations by Emily Fuhrer

BOOK THREE

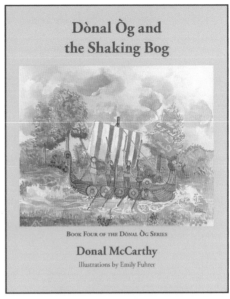

Dònal Òg and
the Shaking Bog

BOOK FOUR OF THE DÒNAL ÒG SERIES

Donal McCarthy

Illustrations by Emily Fuhrer

BOOK FOUR

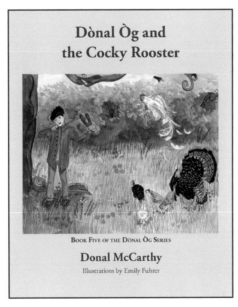

Dònal Òg and
the Cocky Rooster

BOOK FIVE OF THE DÒNAL ÒG SERIES

Donal McCarthy

Illustrations by Emily Fuhrer

BOOK FIVE

Printed in Great Britain
by Amazon

81992114R00025